By, Reading Girls School,
year 7 and year 8 pupils.

Copyright

Contents

About this book

As an author, I regularly visit schools and talk to the pupils about my writing journey and how to best construct a story.
I visited Reading Girls School, virtually, providing inspiration and ideas of what to write. I then encouraged them to write a short story, which has been included in this book.

The short stories in this book have been written by pupils in year 7 and year 8.

Billy's Pets

"Everybody please take a seat."
Said Mrs Xander.
"Urgh, not again!" Billy groaned. Billy never wanted to return from break time. Mrs Xander stared at Billy in a strange way, peering at his jacket.
"Billy, hiding something?"
"no…" Replied Billy worriedly. Billy was hiding his pets from home! That only meant one thing… trouble! He sneaked them in to show his friends. He knew the rules were that there were no pets allowed. "Who would like to show us their first dance for their homework?" She asked. Nobody raise their hands. "Fine then, I'll pick on someone. Ummm…. Billy! Please show us what you have got.
"Oh, no!" thought Billy. Billy started dancing and as hard as he tried to hold on to his pets, they fell to the ground and got revealed! All the children shouted "Poor Billy" as they were his friends. Mrs Xander then

said, "Look what we have here…"
Billy was shaking! What was going
to happen now? But then, Mrs
Xander simply said "I'll forgive you
this time!"
"Now what are we waiting for? Show
us your pets!" The class shouted.
"hooray!" Billy thought that today
was the best school day ever!

By Amy Ogbonna, Year 8.

Change can sometimes be good

You may have never heard of her as she keeps to herself, she finds her own company better than others. She has never been the life of the party and is afraid of others and what they think of her. The girl I have been talking about is Cece Hopson. Cece is the daughter of two fierce and feisty county councillors, Myra and Chandler, who are not afraid to speak their mind. As Cece's parents are very well known in their local area, many citizens are baffled by her personality, they think she doesn't have a brave bone in her body. Little do they know that Cece has a fire simmering in her stomach. The following day at Cece's school, an opportunity arises to take part in the school council but only a certain number of students can be a part of it and must put forward their campaign. Cece heads towards the cafeteria table where the applications are kept as she believes that she has many ideas that could make her school even better when a group of her classmates come up to her. They begin laughing, asking sarcastically why she would even bother sharing her ideas and opinions with the school, she couldn't possibly as she is quiet as a mouse. Cece was rather angry and upset so she quickly snatched the application off the table and walked away with her head down. She was more than ever determined and wanted to show the school that she wasn't a mouse but a strong, brave lion. When she arrived home, the house was silent as both her parents were at council meetings but perfect for writing an important application. Cece sat herself comfortably at her desk, placing her application down on to the table and picked up a pen.

Silence. Cece found that she wasn't particularly good with words and quickly began to feel bored, slowly losing that fire in her stomach. She opened her curtains and began staring out of her bedroom window, getting lost in her own thoughts. BEEP! BEEP! Cece found herself sat down, cross-legged on a pavement, surrounded by towering skyscrapers, loud noises, traffic jams and hordes of people going about their daily lives. Feeling extremely nervous and unsure of her whereabouts, only moments ago she had been completing her school council application. Explanations began running through her mind, had she teleported? was she even there at all? The only logical explanation was that she had drifted off into a daydream. Cece got to her feet and began walking around in what seemed to be a city. While walking around, she heard snippets of conversations coming from the crowds, that seemed strange and were definitely not English. After coming to that conclusion, Cece started asking passers-by if they spoke English. They all shrugged their shoulders in confusion. Cece then noticed rows upon rows of market stalls in the distance, she thought at least one person there would speak some English so she headed that way. As she entered the area of the market stalls, tropical aromas instantly hit her as they were coming from the close by fruit stall. Again, nobody understood her which made her feel very alone and afraid. Suddenly, Cece heard a monkey screeching, Oo Aaa, startled, she looked up at a nearby tree to find a monkey swinging from branch to branch. "Hello said the monkey, would you be able to get me a banana please?" Cece stared in amazement and confusion, was she going crazy or was a monkey really speaking to her?! "Okay," Cece said nervously, in the past she had never needed to talk to people as her parents did that for her. She cautiously walked over to the stall and asked for a banana but the stall owner couldn't understand her, all of sudden a rush of self-doubt overwhelmed her. She shook off her emotions and pointed at the banana and the stall owner instantly understood her. Cece walked away with a beaming smile and her head held high, she then gave the monkey the scrumptious banana and waved goodbye. The monkey had taught her one of his traits, how to be sociable.

As she walked away, Cece noticed the ocean to her right and ran in that direction, she loved the ocean and its beautiful colours. Cece stood looking at the breath-taking views when she noticed a dolphin fin was heading towards the shore, she looked down and saw that a fisherman's net was caught up in its fin. "Excuse me, could you jump into the water and set me free?" cried the dolphin. Cece hesitated, despite not being a confident swimmer, she trusted the dolphin and jumped in fully clothed. After a couple of minutes of struggling with the net, she freed a very grateful dolphin. Cece was felt extremely proud of herself but was beginning to feel hungry after her adventures so she briskly walked back to the centre of the city to find something to satisfy her appetite. Ahead was a small kebab shop on wheels, a few busy roads away so she decided that is where she was going to eat. As she began crossing the roads, Cece heard a booming roar that made her spine shiver and then shrill screams. She headed towards the commotion, pushing her way through the crowds, she found a lion laying on its side. A sudden rush of fear enveloped her body twinned with frustration as nobody was helping the poor animal. Cece gesticulated to one of the curious onlookers to call for veterinarian services and so they quickly pulled out their phone. Cece sat with the injured animal until help arrived. After the lion was dispatched to the nearest animal hospital, the interested crowd cheered for Cece for her extraordinary bravery and courage that they didn't possess. This made her turn crimson red in the cheeks. BANG! Cece opened her eyes slowly, gradually coming back to reality. As she did, Cecel looked around to find herself safely back home not in the busy city. She began to panic as she has spent her time daydreaming instead of writing the application for the school council which was due in tomorrow! Her eyes looked down, to see that her application was filled in and she let out a sigh of relief. The next morning, Cece stood in front of the school with confidence which she thought she would never have and spoke about her ideas that could improve the school. Everyone jumped out of their seats and began applauding her instantly. Cece felt an emotion she had never felt before, pride. That afternoon, while the votes were being counted, she reflected on her daydream and what she had learnt: how to be sociable, trust and courage. Cece was voted onto the school council and not only that, she was elected president!

Remember anything is possible.

By Amera Atta, Year 7.

Could It be me?

Lights flared around me one after another making me squint in their extraordinary brightness. Who am I? Where am I? What is this place around me?

Confused I was. The sky was pitch black around me and roared with rage and anger. The lightning zigzagged in front of me shining with malice. People crowded around with their cameras as if taking a picture for a newspaper report. Vehicles were approaching in all directions there was a police car a few yards away interrogating a couple of teens younger than me. The looked horror-struck and pallid as if they had witnessed the most horrible and gruesome and bloody thing in their entire life. More media trucks and witnessers were emerging out of the dense fog taking their flash cameras and light out and shining it smack at my eyes. Worst of all, in front of me, was an outlined human body marked with chalk piece and the next is impossible to say. I would have been sick if there weren't too many flashlights distracting me. In the distance, I could see a human body. No ordinary one was this It was one which I knew very well. It was none other than my younger sister. Someone had committed a murder. Could that someone be *me*? Compared to me I am in year 10. My name is Hazel. Partly I think my parents named me that because of my hazel eyes compared to my sister she has vivid blue eyes sometimes it just feels as if she is x-raying you and mark my words, she has some tactics with them she can compromise anything she wants making puppy eyes with them.

I was walking ahead of her to school until I reached the school gate that was. I suddenly stopped as I was about to trip over something. I crouched down to see what it was with my crimson gingery brown hair falling forwards dancing to the beat of the wind. It did not even take me a minute to realise that it was none other than someone's phone but that was not the thing. I couldn't stand up. It felt as if I was getting controlled by the phone. I don't know for how long I crouched down there looking like a senseless person but then my sister reached me and started to bang my shoulder.

She started to shout now as there clearly was no sign of response she called, "Hazel! Hazel! Are you alright? Like please do stop ignoring me and answer!"

It took me a strenuous effort to get back to my sense and realise what I was doing as she started to literally hit me on the road.

"OWW.... What do you think you are doing like you are smacking me please do stop!" I snapped at her.

"Well, I would have stopped if you replied to my ear-piercing creams on

the road. Or at the least attended to my patting which actually turned into hitting due to your ignorant behaviour," she contradicted back.
I opened my mouth to argue but realised it had been over 15 minutes and made a run to the school and took the phone with me. I went inside the hall where I normally sit with my friend Alice. She rounded up at me starting what made you so late. I told her about the incident at the gate and she was intrigued; she told me that I should give that phone to a school teacher. I took the phone out and I was speechless.
Actionless. Emotionless. I felt as if I was bloodthirsty. Wanted to avenge something but what for?
Alice nudged me but no response. She patted me but still no response. But Alice being smarter than my sister snatched the phone off me.
All of a sudden, I felt as if the life in my body come back. I started to pant heavily trying to make the word

'Thanks' out which was just impossible.

She replied, "You should actually do something to that phone as a friend I am telling you to break it or do something."

Strangely, I did not reply. It was very abnormal like for me to act like this to my friend. Something was stopping me the same beast swarmed in my stomach again searching to avenge something.

Lessons began the bell rang. It was my sixth lesson today and the last lesson till the end of the day.

I heard a ping my teacher asked our class to check our phones and to make sure they are on silent. I took out a phone thinking it was mine but it wasn't. It was the phone on the road I found. I did not even take a look at it just a glance but my eyes would not come off. I felt a surge of anger malice fury and wanted to see blood. I don't know what was going around me I stormed out but Alice

took the phone out of my hand.
"I told you to give that phone to the school after all it is not yours is it?" She debated.
"Don't get into things that have nothing to do with you" I snapped at her madly.
Something had changed. I have never been so rude to anyone in my life, what is wrong with me?

Mum and Dad said they had to go somewhere to get some certificate and left the house at 7 pm. Only me and Lucy were there we were watching a movie. Until suddenly I hear the same ping I heard in school. I tried to ignore it but somewhere something in my mind chanted 'Look at it! Look at it!'
I couldn't resist my eager anymore I looked at it something rushed into my mind the minute I saw it. I don't know what. All I now saw was revenge anger fury fight for justice. I stared at my sister.

"H...Hazel. Are you all right you seem very creepy please do stop staring at me....."She stuttered.
I laughed a very unusual laugh deep and manly. She screamed or even worse screeched and dashed for the door. I laughed and ran behind her. She was out on the road but I was faster and caught up with her.
That is all I remember so could that someone be me?

By Saru Ganesh, Year 8.

The Struggle of Rich

He saw a light, it seemed like the
tunnel ended here. Maybe everyone
said it true that if you do not eat
food, you will die. He could feel his
end, but he knew that dying was not
the solution here. He looked at the
people, would any of them be kind
enough to give him food, like people
do in the stories he had read.
Rather not, he thought as he looked
at people who were looking hungrier
than he was.
He could not move his legs, his face
turned white and his eyes grew
bigger. He saw two peoples in
human bodies but they were acting
like a bull. A morsel of food was
lying on the ground and two people
near it got on their knees like small
babies' crawl and started it.
The two men started colliding their
heads first and then smartly, one of
them who looked quite skinny than
the other, pushed him in the mud to

make it clear that he had a stone heart and grabbed the morsel.

"mine" he said walking arrogantly in front of him. The muddy man hit his palm on the ground, and he was not looking less than a monster.

He felt them, they were coming for him! He started limping and walking fast. He did not have the strength to run. Maybe it was also true that you should also have vitamin A for good eyesight, he could say that he was getting blind. He could not see a glass bottle lying in front of him and tripping to fall was an easy thing that happened in a flash of light. He felt himself on the ground, he dragged himself away from them. They were quite far away still.

He needed to hide, where? The streets were too narrow. Every door had been locked here. Back in time, they had guards, so every door was open to hide but there was not a single guard here. He thought it was the end but looking around he found

a space just between two houses.
Wide enough for a child like him to
pass through. He squeezed in with
his eyes closed.

But he was not alone there, a long
line was already there to wait in.
More people joined behind him. Is
there any sort of free food that is
been distributed here? Back in time
again, there will be so much food left
that it has to be thrown.
Standing for two hours was not a job
for a boy to do, was it? Suddenly,
everything started to blur in front of
him and then everything black. He
felt himself falling on the hard
ground. The last thing he felt was
someone with soft hands holding
him. His ears had long ago left his
support.
As soon as I was completely lost. I
saw myself: I have golden hair and
white skin. Red lips and blue eyes
made me perfect. I found myself
dressed smartly in a suit and a fake

smile was plastered across my face. It was always like this; his father was too busy to spend time with him. His mother was usually busy with parties. This grand party was different because this was the only day in a whole year where he gets to see his best friend, Chloe.

Soon, Chloe and her dad turned up on the door. She smiled brightly as she saw him but then looked down as she glanced at her father. It was always the same, Chloe's dad did not really love her because the day she was born, her mother left the world. She was a bright girl with pale skin. She had curly black hair and bright red lips. She had the most beautiful brown eyes in the whole world.

I pointed to the emergency room to meet. She nodded and looked away. While all dads and moms would hold their children's hand tightly in the crowded party, Chloe's dad Rob would usually let go of her as soon as he enters the party hall. Chloe founded her legs automatically leading her to the emergency room. The emergency room was the place to hide in case of any attacks on the rich family but for our character Dake and Chloe, it was the meeting spot. She came in and threw her glass slippers and they hit the wall. Her bare feet were all red now. It must be painful to wear glass or any types of girls' slippers. Then all I knew or could remember was the shooting from the guns. The next thing I knew was the heavy knocks from the scared people who were running like ants here and there. I did not open the door and neither did let Chloe who was brave enough to do it. After about half an hour, everything was silent. We opened the door. Everyone there was……dead and covered in blood. My dad, uncle and….'thud' Chloe fell down on her knees and on the floor. I spotted the criminals and ran away in the darkness of night. I ran. I fell. I was running when I entered a house, their owner was dead in my house, the guard was lying on the floor. I ran and that is when I found a door in the house which was luckily opened. I entered. I left the door open in panic. I ran and the men followed.

'aaaahhhhhh' I screamed.

Lying on the bed, I read the board ORPHANAGE.

Right, the perspective has to change now. Hi, I am the warden. I am young with my black hairs always tied in a bun. My black eyes and dry red lips complete my look. I found that little boy in that smelly and very narrow street. Lucky him, I found him, a member of an orphanage. If anyone else was the fortunate one, he would have been a slave or something. I entered the room hearing that deafening voice. I asked.

'Maybe' he replied with a shaky

voice.

'Water' I offered kindly in my best polite voice I can manage.

He stared at me. Finally, took the glass and gulped one sip.

'Okay, stop drinking if you want to die peacefully and less painfully'

'What?' He asked in a weak voice and he nearly fell on the bed.

I controlled him and answered him 'You are dying quickly; on the bottle, it says 20 minutes after the drink the eyes see darkness before them. Very weak you are. Well, I want the password for the diamond locker in your bank. Before you say I don't know, I have heard your dad speaking to the manager that only you can open it. If you give me the password within 5 minutes, saving you will be an easy job for me with this medicine'.

That poor and dumb boy replied very foolishly 'I don't know!!!!'

Well, he replied with this answer repeatedly and requested.

'Please, do not kill me, I swear, I have no idea about what the password would be'

5 minutes passed. First, he fell down on the bed. White fluid started to drip from his mouth and his eyes closed. I never expected that I would have to kill a boy with my own hands. If only those men would have done their job correctly and blackmailed him. I do not have that much patience in these cases.

By Harshita Singh, Year 8.

The Emerald Culprit

The beginning!!

There was once a land far away far from our universes.

There was a land called IV land-it was named by the first people who came to that planet-with the people with the elements of water, wind, earth and fire. Their names were Aqua- she had waterpowers, Igni-he had firepowers, Ventus- she had wind power and Terra-she had earth power. They all lived in harmony until the darkness took over IV land. Therefore, the four elements banished it to the darkest part of IV land. No one was afraid of the darkness again.

The Other World

After the old elements died, the people needed to choose the new elements. They looked for years, months and centuries. They could not find anything. But one day they found them. They were human but they could turn back to elves because they turned in to human because they need to hide them from people from the IV land. They were elves but they turned them human so that they looked like them so they didn't get spotted.

Introduction

Katty-she was 16 and she was a trainee doctor. She lived in 23 Dawn Street in a little apartment and she had a dog called Dizzy who was 1 year old. She had the power of the earth. She had blond hair and blue eyes.

May - she was 15. She was an Olympic swimmer and she had a pet fish called Finly. She had the power of water. She lived in Poland. She lived in a little house near a lake where she practised and she had light brown skin as brown as chocolate and had brown eyes and blue extensions like the lake near her house. She lived in Jamaica. James- he was 16 and he worked as a librarian. His pet was a bird called Speedy and he lived in a flat near a forest where he practised his powers. He had black hair and brown eyes. He lived in Jamaica.

Stacy –she was 15 and she worked as a dog walker. She had a pet cat called Cupcake and she had fire powers. She lived near a park and that is where she practised her powers. She had red hair and freckles. She lived in London.

The IV

The dragons took their elements and silently they went out of the earth and went off into space. They were flying for miles and in the end, they reached IV land. They took them to the elves and they placed them on a soft bed outside where they said their spell. They banged the drums and then fire came. They said the spell but before they could do anything they needed to put something in their body so they couldn't feel anything. They needed to make them drink a special flower so they carefully gave it to them. Then they went into a deep sleep. They carried on with the spell "dryadalis". They turned in to elves.

When they woke up!!!

They woke up and tried to get up. They were very confused and frightened. They tried getting out but they could not move-the magic potion made sure they did not move. The dragons came one by one. They said 'We will train them first thing in the morning. Give us our elements in the woods. The only

one that is not is the one with water.
She will be in a waterfall.

INTRO of the dragons

Fire –Augug
Water- Cataracta
Earth-Petram
Wind-Turbinis Vasti

Training

They started early in the morning.
They woke up tired,
"Where are we? I think we are going
to die. Why? I was so young too,"
"Die? You are not going to die. Why
would we do that James?" said one
of the elves. They made all the elves
and dragons. The best thing was
that it did not take long for them to
calm them and when I mean calm
down, I mean James, but he calmed
down after an hour or two. The girls
loved the dragons and trained
harder than you ever could imagine
and finally they were ready for their
first battle. But of course, they
needed practice so they could win.

They splashed and they sploshed and they banged and NOW IT IS TIME they won!!!!! Everyone was happy about how much they tried. It was amazing they wanted ice cream but they were a bit weird. They had never tried it before. It was so yummy. They finally went to sleep.

The Emerald City

They went on a road trip to the east far from the IV land. They told them the story of the emerald. The people loved anything green. One day they saw emerald everywhere. They started to build homes and all they had was emerald. They would pay money with emerald, their clothes were made of them. They loved it but now someone was stealing them. It was up to you to find that elf or whatever it is. They finally reached Emerald City. "It is soo green is this veg garden that was funny come on, "laughed

James. "It is not funny James," said Katty, angrily.

"Guys, let's stop fighting, we should just look," said May happily. They went to the mayor's house. Her name was Emily Emerald. Her great, great grandfather found that place. "Hi y'all. This place is where greatness happens and nothing else. You guys judge us just because you have powers and it doesn't mean you can be rude to us, ok? "She said happily. "She is weird," said Stacy confusedly. "Don't be so rude Stacy. Even though she was so rude to us does not mean she we have to be rude even though she was. Ok, we are on a mission," she said angrily. They went out of the room and Stacy saw something in the distance. She went and whispered to them and said I think I have found the green robber. They all slowly used powers and caught him and he was James. He took it because he was thinking

that they did not deserve to
have the emeralds. They locked him
up and their mission was complete.
Their task and know they were the
four guys. What is that black thing in
the sky? It is heading to the IV land.
Oh, no ……. to be continued !!!!

By Ayra Sultan, Year 7.

Fight-Fright-Freedom

It was all around me. Darkness. Not a soul to be found. Shrill screams echoed constantly piercing my ears. I couldn't move. I couldn't breathe. Suddenly, I saw a sign... It was blurred out but there was small writing next to it. I unleashed myself and broke free from the chains that heavily held me down. Scrambling up, I rushed to the wall grabbing the screws that hadn't been put in properly. It read-

WERE WATCHING. WE ALWAYS HAVE BEEN...

The sign was still wet and dripped down the walls but it was written in the worst thing imaginable

BLOOD.

I ventured on, fright surging through my veins until I felt a shudder crawl

down my spine as something, possibly someone grabbed my right shoulder. The thought of the blood-curdling sign rang in my head as my petrified-self ran. Unknowingly, I plunged myself deeper into the darkness ahead. For I would rather face that than whatever or *whoever* grasped my shoulder. Suddenly, the door opened and the wind blew so hard, that I struggled to stay put and fell. My head hit the floor and it pained to open my eyes. The last thing I could remember was seeing blood – a lot of it - gushing out of someone. Me.

I woke up and only saw darkness around me. My heartbeat faster than ever before and I felt as if it was going to fall out. I eventually calmed down because I realized I was on a bed and I had a bandage around my head but I could feel the blood seeping out because I was covered in it. The bedroom had a mattress and a blue blanket which I was sleeping on and it seemed It belonged to someone because there were several pictures and photos and paintings of family. I was extremely shocked at how I could have got here and thought it was a dream. I finally decided to get u and have a look around.

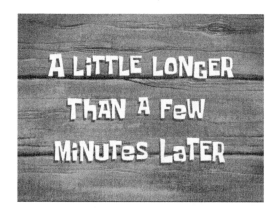

I was on the swing wondering how I got here, wondering who would be nice enough to help me at such a dark and gloomy place. And I ever thought I would say this but-
"My little baby girl, welcome home."
I didn't understand, my mom died ages ago, giving birth to me but when I turned around, I couldn't believe what I saw-

By Ayat Mirza, Year 7.

Wild escape

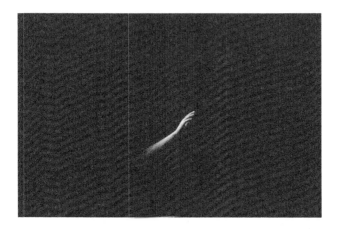

It was the year 1939. *A year which I thought would be like any other but I was very wrong, it was the year that everything changed.*
Mamma and Pappa were downstairs listening to the daily news and I was upstairs playing with my dolls. That day was very vague as I never expected that it was at this moment that my life would change.
Mamma came to tuck me into bed. She looked ever so pale and her

eyes were all puffed and red as if she had been crying. I asked her what was the matter but she just said hay fever. I did not continue pestering her but I knew that something was not right. I went to bed dreaming of new worlds and new adventures, unaware of what was happening outside at this very moment.

The next day, mamma and pappa called me and my brother, Max, downstairs and said that they had to talk about something serious. There was a look on their faces, very stern and serious, which I had never seen before. I knew something was wrong and my heart was racing out of my chest. "As you know, Germany is now at war and we believe that they are going to be taking people like us to something called a concentration camp, so we are really sorry but we are all going to have to pack our bags and leave as soon as possible." My mind was churning with so many questions and emotions. "Why us?" and "Concentration camp" were swirling in my mind like when mamma cooks her broth. Pappa looked at my face and said: "We are Jews, and we can't take a risk losing you in a concentration camp, you are too dear to us and as long as we are your parents, we have a duty to protect you." This made me feel warm but cold at the same time. I could not imagine leaving Germany and all of my memories here. Although, a part of me was also excited because this was going to be an adventure never written in the books.

We packed our bags very lightly with just the essentials such as clothes and one toy. Mamma said that she will buy us everything when we are at our new house. We left as quick as we could and boarded our train to Switzerland and then from there, we were going to take a boat to

England. When we were boarding the train, I could see a cart full of women and men being forced and pushed onto carriages like animals by these smartly dressed soldiers. This made me feel very cold inside and I grabbed Mamma's arm for comfort. She gave me a reassuring squeeze and said that we were going to be safe. When we were moving, I felt very drowsy and went into the deepest sleep I felt like I ever went into. It was boiling hot despite there being snow outside. I did not feel like eating but Max was helping himself to the buffet. He was scoffing all the pastries, desserts and sausages he could find. That was the last thing I could remember before I blacked out.

When I woke up, I felt the world spinning and my head felt like it was going to burst out. I could hear the murmuring of Mamma and Pappa but there was another voice too, slightly deeper than Pappas. I opened my eyes to see a smartly dressed man. I thought it was one of those soldier men and began screaming, "Mamma, Pappa run, they are going to take us away!" Mamma came and pacified me. She assured me it was just the doctor and that there was nothing for me to worry about. "Pneumonia, not a very severe case but if not treated can be dangerous but we can provide you with the medicine" is all I heard until I blacked out again.

Later in the day, I was awake and I was in this new room. It was slightly smaller than our house in Germany but it was very cosy. Mamma and Pappa had already decorated the room. It was very quick; I wonder how they did it in a few hours? "You have been sleeping for 3 whole days young lady!" and then she chuckled "I thought you might have been in a coma; we were absolutely worried sick!"

After a few days, I gained my

strength and wanted to explore this new place called the Cotswolds. It was surrounded by countryside and green grasses. There were many local animals which I had never actually seen before as we were in the city. Life in the countryside was very serine.

Everybody is close-knit and besides, I have what I need. I felt a pang about all my friends and life in Germany but I know I am in a better place with my family. We had a big adventure-a wild escape.

By Maryam Ali, Year 8.

Testimonial

Our pupils were fascinated to hear from a 'real life' author! Kath kept all our pupils enthralled with her talk, which covered topics such as how to write a story, the key components of a story and using a random word generator. She was bombarded with questions which were dealt with extremely patiently. An excellent virtual session!

Steph Smith, English Teacher, Reading Girls' School.

Other books by Kath Kirkland

The Chocolate Thief – junior read. Available in paperback through your local bookstore, and on e-book.

Billy likes chocolate. All he eats is chocolate. A chocolate thief starts stealing all the chocolate in the town. Billy is accused of the thefts by his classmates, the head-teacher and even the police.

Who is the chocolate thief and will Billy be able to eat chocolate again?

Will the police catch the chocolate thief who is destroying the lives of many children?

How to contact Kath Kirkland

If you have any questions for Kath, you can contact her in several ways or follow her on Social Media.

Sign up to the newsletter via the website - www.kathkirklandauthor.co.uk
Email – kathkirklandauthor@gmail.com
Twitter – @kathauthor
Facebook – https://www.facebook.com/kathkirklandauthor/
Instagram – https://www.instagram.com/kmkauthor/
LinkedIn – https://www.linkedin.com/in/kathkirklandauthor/

Kath is always happy to attend schools to inspire the pupils to write. She is also available for book readings and book signings and to attend events and club meetings. Please contact her for details.

Printed in Great Britain
by Amazon